TONY BRADMAN

DILLY

and the
Cup Final

Illustrated by Susan Hellard

Mammoth

First published in 1997 by Mammoth,
an imprint of Reed International Books Ltd,
Michelin House, 81 Fulham Road, London SW3 6RB
and Auckland and Melbourne

Text copyright © 1997 Tony Bradman
Illustrations copyright © 1997 Susan Hellard

ISBN 0 7497 3009 9

10 9 8 7 6 5 4 3 2 1

A CIP catalogue record for this book is available at the British Library

Printed in Great Britain by Cox and Wyman Ltd, Reading, Berkshire

Contents

1 Dilly and the video camera   1

2 Dilly and the school report   16

3 Dilly and the cup final   31

4 Dilly and the sleepover party   46

For Jamie – fame at last!
T.B.

For Sheffield United – fame at last!
S.H.

1 Dilly and the video camera

'Wow, look at *that*!' said my little brother Dilly as we walked into the shopping cavern. He dashed over to the toy store and gazed longingly through the window. 'Can I have something, Father? Please?'

'I don't think so, Dilly,' said Father, and kept walking. I did the same and, a few moments later, Dilly came scampering after us.

'But *why* won't you buy me a toy, Father?' he said in that whiny, irritating voice he puts on. 'I haven't been naughty today, have I?'

'Not yet, anyway,' I said. 'But, then, it's still pretty early.'

'Drop dead, Dorla,' snapped Dilly, turning and giving me one of his extra-mean-narrow-eyed-evil stares. I stuck my tongue out at him.

'Oh, for heaven's sake, you two, don't start,' said Father without slowing down. 'Actually, Dilly, there are several reasons. In the first place, you've already got cupboards full of toys you hardly ever play with.'

'That's because he's broken most of them,' I muttered. 'On purpose.'

'It's not true!' squealed Dilly indignantly.

'And in the second place,' said Father, giving me a look, 'we just don't have enough money to buy everything you ask for. Besides, you wouldn't want to be spoilt, would you?' Dilly opened his mouth to reply, but Father held up a paw. 'You needn't answer that. Ah, here we are.'

Father strode through the doors of a large shop and we followed him.

'Hi, there!' said a young dinosaur. 'How may I help you this morning?'

Dilly was gawping at the stuff that was for sale. There were TVs, CD-players and walk-o-saur, dino-phones, computers and computer games, and hundreds of other interesting things.

'Hello,' said Father. 'I'd like to buy a video camera.'

Dilly whirled round the instant he heard Father say the word 'buy'. He put his paws on his hips and gave Father an even more powerful extra-mean-narrow-eyed-evil stare than the version he'd used on me.

Father didn't seem to feel Dilly's eyes burning into his neck, though. He chose a camera and paid for it. Then we left and headed for the dino-car.

Dilly didn't say a word. He stomped off ahead of Father and me, STOMP, STOMP, STOMP, and waited by the dino-car. His tail was quivering and he was tapping his foot impatiently. He looked cross.

'OK, Dilly,' sighed Father. 'What's the problem now?'

'How come *you* get what you want,' said Dilly grumpily, 'and *I* don't?'

'It's very simple really, Dilly,' said Father as we drove off. 'Your mother and I are the grown-ups, so we decide how to spend our money. You and Dorla aren't the grown-ups, I'm afraid, so . . . you don't.'

'Well, it's not fair,' Dilly muttered. 'One day I'll be rich, and then I'll be able to buy whatever I want. Just you wait and see, Father!'

'I won't hold my breath, Dilly,' laughed Father. 'But if you do think of a way to make a fortune, I hope you'll let your old dad in on the secret.'

Dilly snorted, and snootily turned up his snout.

He stayed in mega-sulk mode for the rest of the morning. His mood didn't change until after lunch when Father started doing some filming with the video camera. Dilly couldn't help himself. He was fascinated.

He loosened up gradually. He asked Father questions about the camera and posed with Swampy, his pet swamp lizard. Then he insisted that Father film him playing Attack of the Vicious Killer Alien Dinosaurs.

Then Dilly got excited.

And whenever he gets excited, Dilly behaves badly. By the time he went to bed later that evening, Dilly's behaviour had been extremely bad, even by his low standards. We had proof of it for once, too.

Father had filmed everything with the video camera.

There were lots of shots of Dilly being naughty, and Mother telling him off. You could hear Father on the soundtrack doing his share of the telling off as well. And, as you might expect, there was plenty of shouting.

'Oh, Dilly, aren't you ashamed of yourself?' said Mother the next day when she was watching the video with Dilly and me. Father was at work.

'No, Mother,' said Dilly. He sounded surprised at the suggestion.

'Well, you should be, you tyke,' said Mother. Then she laughed. 'Mind you, it's like a teach-yourself guide to bad behaviour for little dinosaurs. Your friends would probably pay a fortune for tips like these.'

'Do you really think so, Mother?' said Dilly, suddenly alert.

'Oh, yes,' said Mother. 'You could call it *101 Ways To Drive Your Parents Crazy*. Although it would definitely end up being banned. As far as grown-ups are concerned, this is worse than any horror movie!'

I knew Mother was only being funny, but Dilly looked thoughtful. He has occasionally led some of his friends astray. Now I wondered if Mother's joke had made him think of doing it on a much larger scale . . .

I decided to watch him, just in case.

At first, I couldn't seem to catch him doing anything out of the ordinary. Of course, that only made me even more suspicious. As you know, Dilly can be very, very cunning. But he finally gave himself away.

One morning, as we were leaving for school, Dilly suddenly ducked into the living-room. Mother was already outside, starting the dino-car. And when Dilly emerged, his book-bag was bulging a bit more than usual.

'I could have sworn I put the video I made under the TV,' said Father that evening, scratching his head. 'You haven't taken it, have you, Dilly?'

'What, me?' said Dilly quickly, doing his best to look angelic. 'No, Father, I haven't. Why would I do something like that?'

And, amazingly enough, Father believed him!

But, then, Father hadn't seen Dilly huddled with his little friends in the quietest corner of the school playground. They had been giggling and passing something between them. I had a good idea what it was, too.

Father hadn't heard Dilly talking to himself, either. I had, because I'd crept up and listened at Dilly's bedroom door. 'One, two, three,' he'd been murmuring happily, and there had been a light, chinking sound.

I had a good idea what he'd been counting, as well.

Things continued like this for a couple of weeks. Mother and Father didn't realise what was going on, although there were plenty of clues. For instance, there was the epidemic of bad behaviour among Dilly's friends.

'You didn't tell me Dudley had been grounded by his parents, Dilly,' said Mother as we were walking home after school one day. 'And what's this I've been hearing about Denzil, and Delbert, and Darryl?'

'Er . . . they've all been grounded too, Mother,' said Dilly.

'Well, I don't know, Dilly,' said Mother, and laughed. 'Maybe you're not as badly behaved as your father and I think. Your school friends certainly seem to be getting up to a lot more than you at the moment.'

Dilly just smiled sweetly. In fact, he looked so incredibly pleased with himself that I felt like saying something to Mother there and then. But I managed not to. I knew I would have to wait for just the right moment.

It came the very next morning.

'Father, are we going to the shopping

cavern today?' said Dilly.

'No, Dilly,' said Father. 'We are not going to the shopping cavern, and I do wish you'd drop the subject. That's the fourth time you've asked me since breakfast. And what on earth have you got in your pocket?'

Father was peering at Dilly's dungarees. I'd noticed it too. Something was dragging one side of them down, and making Dilly lean over.

'Er . . . nothing, Father,' he said, and limped off towards the door.

'Hold it right there, Dilly,' said Father sternly, his suspicions roused. 'I think I'd like to see this *nothing* that looks as if it weighs a couple of tons.'

Father held out his paw. Dilly gulped, then eased a packed purse from his pocket. It slipped, landed on the floor with a THUD! and split open. Lots of shiny coins rolled around our feet. Father was rather taken aback.

'But where did you get all this money, Dilly?' he said.

'Well, I . . .' Dilly mumbled.

'Why don't you ask him about the naughty video, Father?' I said.

That did it. Dilly flashed me an I'll-get-you-back-for-this glare, then . . . he opened his mouth and let rip with an ultra-special, 150-mile-per-hour super-scream, the kind that tells us he knows he's been found out.

Once Dilly had finally stopped screaming, Father extracted the truth from him. Dilly confessed that he *had* been renting the video to his little friends. They had watched it secretly and learned plenty of new tricks.

But Father wasn't very cross. He seemed to find it funny, especially the fact that Mother was embarrassed about it being her idea. Father did say Dilly was grounded, though, and that he would have to return the money.

'What . . . *all* of it?' said Dilly glumly.

'Every penny,' said Father. 'Just be grateful I don't make you call your friends' parents on the dino-phone and apologise for what you've done. Mind you, I feel we ought to do *something* to make it up to them.'

'Why don't you rent them the video, Father?' said Dilly eagerly. 'You could call it *101 Ways To Tell Off Your Naughty Little Dinosaur*. I bet you'd make your fortune, and then you could buy me lots of toys . . .'

'I don't think so, Dilly,' said Father, smiling. 'Nice try, though.'

'It was, wasn't it?' said Dilly, smiling too.

Then he skipped happily into the garden to play.

2 Dilly and the school report

I heard something a while ago that made me feel *so* excited. Dilly and I were due to be given our school reports, and my teacher hinted mine would be *very* good. I couldn't wait to tell Mother on the way home.

It was impossible to get through to her, though.

'I'm sorry, Dorla, what were you saying?' she said.

'Mrs Drake told me . . .' I began, and didn't get any further.

'Dilly, what are you doing *now*?' Mother called out suddenly. 'That's somebody's garden, you know, and I don't think they'll be happy about you trampling on their flowers. Now, climb back over this wall instantly.'

'Don't want to,' said Dilly. 'Not going to. Na-na-nee-na-na,' he sang, and stuck his tongue out. For some reason he'd been really awful recently.

'Right!' said Mother, and we had the usual embarrassing scene, with Mother telling

Dilly off loudly, then dragging him home by the paw.

I trudged up to my room and settled down to do some serious sulking. I felt totally depressed. 'Looks like you only get any attention round here by being a badly behaved little brat,' I muttered darkly to myself.

Then I thought about what I'd just said. If being badly behaved was what it took to get noticed, then maybe that was what I had to do . . . I'd had more than enough of being the good one in the family.

OK, I decided. From this moment on, Mother and Father would see a completely different Dorla. A difficult, demanding, *devastating* Dorla . . .

I revealed the new me at dinner the same evening.

'What's wrong, Dorla?' said Mother. 'You haven't eaten your swamp greens. And there's your favourite for dessert, marsh-mud pie.'

'I don't want my swamp greens,' I said. 'They're *disgusting*.'

Then I pushed my plate away, hard. It bumped into the gravy jug, which toppled over, sending gravy splashing across the table. It dripped on Father's lap, while the jug rolled off on to the floor and . . . SMASHED!

'Dorla, what a naughty thing to do!' said Mother, surprised. 'Now go and fetch a cloth to soak up this mess, and be quick about it!'

'No, I won't!' I yelled. 'And *you* can't make me.'

Two bottom jaws dropped in shock, and it

was so funny I nearly burst out laughing on the spot. Mother and Father couldn't believe I was being badly behaved. Dilly's face was an absolute picture as well.

Mother and Father managed to pull themselves together. They gave me a stiff telling off and sent me to my room.

After that, I went from bad to worse. I wouldn't do what I was told, I threw tantrums, I talked back, I acted as if the TV belonged to me . . . To cut a long story short, I did all the stuff Dilly has been doing for years.

He just couldn't compete. I know him so well, I could tell when he was about to misbehave and I made sure I beat him to it. Soon Mother and Father were only giving him as much attention as they usually give me.

I was getting much more.

'But why are you behaving like this,

Dorla?' said Mother one evening. She'd been with me for *ages*. 'Are there any problems at school?'

'No,' I said, as cool as you like, turning the page in my comic.

Mind you, I was telling the truth. Even though I was getting up to mischief at home, in class I was still the same well-behaved, hard-working Dorla. I didn't want to risk ruining my report, did I?

So my little plot was going nicely, and I was feeling fairly smug. But Dilly isn't stupid, and I should have realised he would work out what I was up to. Although I could never have imagined how he would retaliate.

Incredible as it might seem, Dilly started being . . . *well behaved*.

'Shall I tidy my toy cupboard, Mother?' he asked one afternoon, with a swamp-butter-wouldn't-melt-in-his-mouth look. I was about to throw a tantrum because Father had told me it was time I turned off the TV.

Those two bottom jaws dropped again. Mother was always trying to get Dilly to clear up his toy cupboard, and he never, ever did.

'I beg your pardon, Dilly?' squeaked Mother at last.

'I'd like to tidy my toy cupboard,' Dilly said patiently. 'I also wondered if there was anything else I could do around the house for you,' he burbled brightly. 'I mean, I've got lots of time before I begin my . . . *homework.*'

That last little touch almost made me smile. For a second I thought Dilly might have overplayed it. The thought of him actually doing any homework without being ordered to was beyond belief.

But he *did* do it, *and* he tidied his toy cupboard, and by the end of the afternoon he had become a completely different kind of pest. He kept trailing after Mother and Father, asking them what they wanted him to do!

And this time *I* couldn't compete. I think Mother and Father were so pleased one of us was being good, they chose not to see that it was just Dilly being devious. Pretty soon he was getting all the attention again.

'Well, Dilly, I must say this makes a very pleasant change,' said Mother as Dilly helped her load the dishwasher, which was something I usually did. 'I only wish another little dinosaur I know would be as nice . . .'

I didn't hang around to hear any more. Later that evening, Dilly and I happened to pass each other on the stairs. He was going up and I was coming down. We both paused. Our eyes met and locked.

Dilly gave me a cocky smile.

At that moment I was very tempted to go back to being good. Thinking of new ways to be naughty the whole time had turned out to be a lot harder than it looked. I was definitely beginning to run short of ideas.

I didn't enjoy the tellings-off, either, and I couldn't forget them as easily as Dilly does. To be honest, I'd realised I didn't have Dilly's talent for bad behaviour, and the whole situation was making me feel uncomfortable.

I refused to give in, though. I didn't want Dilly to get one over me. No, this was something I'd have to follow through to the bitter end.

'Your move, Dorla,' said Dilly.

'It is, isn't it?' I said in my most confident who's-the-brilliant-big-sister-around-here? voice. Dilly's smile faded and was replaced by an uncertain expression. I pushed past him and carried on downstairs.

So I stuck with the bad behaviour. I went for the simple stuff, mostly, like generally being awkward at every opportunity, and throwing tantrums whenever Mother and Father wouldn't let me do what I wanted.

That meant Dilly was forced to stick with the good behaviour too, and I soon noticed something *very* interesting. It seemed Dilly was having just as much trouble with being well behaved as I was with being naughty.

In fact, the strain was really beginning to tell.

'I think you'd better have your bath and go to bed earlier than usual tonight, Dilly,' Mother said to him one evening. 'We've promised to be at Aunt Dimpla's house by nine o'clock tomorrow and it's a long drive.'

I held my breath. It was the kind of thing that would normally make Dilly throw a tantrum, especially as it would mean he'd miss his current favourite noisy and violent cartoon, *The Dino Rangers*.

Dilly sat utterly motionless in front of the TV. He was muttering, and I could see he was trying to keep himself under control. It was obviously a tough battle, and I felt sure he was close to losing it. But he didn't.

'OK, Mother,' he said at last in a weak, wobbly voice. 'Just coming.'

Reluctantly, he turned off the TV and slowly trudged upstairs. Blast, I thought. If he could hold out against *that* kind of pressure, I didn't have much hope of winning. I was almost at breaking point myself.

There was one final twist to come, however. Dilly had made a fatal error. He had become a changed dinosaur at school as well as at home, as we discovered when Dilly and I were given our school reports.

'This *is* a suprise,' said Mother when she'd read them. 'I'll admit I wasn't expecting your report to be good, Dorla, not with the way you've been behaving recently. But it's the best one you've ever had. Well done!'

'Er . . . what about mine, Mother?' said Dilly, nervously.

'That's a bit of a surprise, too,' Mother replied, sounding a little dazed. 'I was expecting your report to be much the same as usual, but it's *much* better! I never thought I'd say this, Dilly – but keep it up!'

Mother's words had a dramatic effect on Dilly. I think he suddenly saw years of good behaviour stretching ahead of him, and just couldn't bear it.

'I . . . I don't think I can, Mother!' he wailed.

Then his face crumpled and, that's right, you guessed it . . . he let rip with an ultra-special, 150-mile-per-hour super-scream, the kind that says he's finally had enough, and leaves Mother looking very confused.

Of course, everything had to come out after that. Dilly said he'd only been good because I had been naughty, and I said I'd only been naughty because I'd been fed up with him being awful and getting all the attention.

Then Dilly said he'd only been awful recently because I'd been doing so well at school that Mother and Father hardly took notice of him any more. I couldn't believe it – we had been feeling the same about each other!

'What a pair!' said Mother at last, laughing and giving us a hug. 'It's a good job your Father and I love you *equally*. Now, if I promise to give you both plenty of attention, do you think we could get back to normal?'

Dilly and I nodded eagerly. And pretty soon life was more relaxed than it had been for quite a while. Mind you, I was glad it had all happened . . .

If you ask me, it always pays to keep your parents on their toes!

3 Dilly and the cup final

'Hey, terrific, Father,' said Dilly with an enormous grin. We had just arrived at the sports centre where Dilly and I play football on Saturdays. 'If you're the referee this morning, my team will *definitely* win!'

The sports centre runs lots of football teams for young dinosaurs. I'm in the top team for my age group. Dilly is in a team with some friends, and he adores football. There is *one* problem, though . . . he can't stand losing.

In fact, Dilly will do almost anything to win. So, when I heard Father offering to referee Dilly's game, I had an awful feeling there might be trouble. Father, you see, is pretty strict about sticking to the rules.

'Oh, Dilly,' laughed Mother. 'That's not how it works.'

'No, it *isn't*,' I said. Dilly gave me a dirty look, but I ignored it.

'Your mother and Dorla are right, Dilly,' said Father. 'You shouldn't expect me to give your team special treatment. That wouldn't be fair.'

'But I thought you'd want us to win, Father,' said Dilly. His grin had vanished and he was scowling. 'You hate it when your team is beaten.'

'Maybe I do,' said Father in that I-must-keep-my-patience tone of his. 'Mind you, I've had to get used to it. And I certainly wouldn't want them to win by cheating. Mark my words, Dilly, no game is ever *that* important.'

'Well, we're going to win today, Father,'

said Dilly fiercely, his arms folded and his scowl deepening. 'Whether you help us or not.'

'Whatever you say, Dilly,' sighed Father. 'Just behave yourself, OK?'

'Huh!' grunted Dilly, and trotted away. Uh-oh, I thought . . .

My game started before Dilly's, and Mother and Father watched me until it was time for Dilly's kick-off. Father had to go, but Mother stayed until my game finished. Then we went to see how Dilly was getting on.

'What's the score?' Mother asked Dilly's team coach.

'Still nil-nil, thank goodness,' the coach replied. 'Although we're lucky not to be losing. And, er . . . I'm afraid Dilly's been rather naughty.'

Dilly had tripped up the opposition striker. Father had seen Dilly do it and shown him the yellow card. There were only a few minutes left now, and Dilly's team were defending desperately.

That same striker broke through again, and soon she just had the goalkeeper to beat. Suddenly a small green figure appeared from nowhere. It was Dilly. He came bustling across, and trod on the little striker's tail!

She went down with a yelp of pain. Father arrived on the scene, blew his whistle with a piercingly loud PEEP! and pointed to the penalty spot. Sternly, he signalled Dilly to approach him. Dilly trudged over.

'OK, Dilly,' said Father. 'What have you got to say for yourself?'

'Nothing, Father,' mumbled Dilly.

'Very well,' said Father. 'I'm sending you off.'

He took out his red card and held it up.

'You . . . you can't do that!' spluttered Dilly.

But Father's faint smile said he could.

Dilly was furious. He swivelled on his heel and marched from the muddy pitch. He stood on the touchline, his paws thrust deep into the pockets of his long, baggy shorts, and silently . . . *fumed*.

Father checked that the little striker was OK. Her tail did look a bit bent. But I'm glad to say she was fine, and she wanted to take the penalty herself. She placed the ball on the penalty spot and walked back.

Everyone went quiet, and the goalkeeper waited tensely.

Father glanced in Dilly's direction – and it was lucky he did. Dilly had opened his mouth ready to deliver an ultra-special, 150-mile-per-hour super-scream . . . which would definitely have put the little striker off.

It would probably have frightened the goalkeeper totally out of his wits too. But that wouldn't have mattered so long as the striker made a mess of her kick. Dilly must have thought it was worth the risk.

Father, however, had no intention of letting him get away with it.

'Dilly . . .' he said, 'do the words *life-time ban* mean anything to you?'

Dilly shut his mouth with a SNAP! The little striker stepped up, took the penalty, and scored! Father blew the whistle for the end of the game. Dilly's team had lost one-nil, and he wasn't a happy dinosaur at all.

'I *hate* you, Father,' Dilly muttered on the way home. More than once.

Father was rather grumpy too, and it looked like we were in for a pretty bad weekend. But then something amazing happened which made Father much more cheerful. Dino-Town United actually won a game!

When the score came up on TV that afternoon, Father was so surprised he stopped shouting in the middle of giving Dilly yet another telling-off. Mother said the announcer must have got it wrong. But she hadn't.

To be honest, none of us can understand why Father is such a fan of Dino-Town United. As far as we can make out, they've never won any trophies, and they seem to lose most of their matches.

Dino-Town United won their next match, and the next one, and the one after that. In fact, they were on a real winning streak, and by the end of the season they had reached the Cup Final!

Father was delighted, of course. He was even more pleased when he managed to get four tickets for the game. This was Dino-Town United's big chance, and the whole of Dino-Town was supporting the team.

Nobody was rooting for them as much as Father, though.

The great day came at last. Mother and Father woke us early and we set off for the stadium. There were thousands and thousands of dinosaurs heading in the same direction, and we had to queue for ages at the gate.

The noise inside was tremendous. We had seats right behind one of the goals and Mother, Dilly and I joined in all the fun. We sang, we chanted, and we did our bit in every dinosaur wave. But Father was very quiet.

'Look at Father, Mother,' I said, giving Mother a nudge.

I don't think I've ever seen Father so tense. He was wearing his Dino-Town United bobble hat and scarf, and he was sitting next to Dilly with his paws clasped tightly together. He might even have been *praying* . . .

Mother rolled her eyes, and she and I smiled at each other.

'Relax, dear,' she said to Father. 'You won't enjoy it otherwise.'

'Who said anything about enjoying it?' Father replied grimly. 'Nothing could be as important as this. It's the most vital match in the history of Dino-Town United. Correction, the *universe*. I want my team to *win*.'

Dilly didn't say anything. He did give Father a questioning look though, the kind that usually comes before one of those I-thought-you-said speeches of his. But just then the whistle went, and the game began.

It was an incredibly thrilling match. Play flowed from end to end, and with only a few seconds to go, Father's team were two-one in the lead. Then disaster struck. Dino-Town United gave away a penalty!

Father held his head in his paws and moaned. Then he suddenly sat upright and looked at Dilly. We knew exactly what Father was thinking.

Dare he ask Dilly to use his scream? I could see from his face Father desperately wanted to, and that he *didn't* want to, all at the same time. Dilly just sat there with his arms folded, enjoying Father's agony.

'Yes, Father?' Dilly said smugly at last. 'You wouldn't want me to give your team *special treatment*, would you? I mean, that wouldn't be fair, would it?'

'I, er . . .' Father mumbled, looking to Mother for help.

'Oh, no, leave me out of it,' she said, laughing. 'This is between you two.'

The opposition striker was walking back from the ball. The Dino-Town United goalkeeper waited, and an eerie hush fell over the whole stadium.

It was too much for Father.

'OK, I know it's wrong,' he said, 'but this is a special occasion, and I'd never forgive myself if they lost in extra time. What's the deal, Dilly?'

'You have to raise my pocket money,' said Dilly, smiling wickedly. Father nodded. 'Buy me a complete Dino-Town United outfit.' Father nodded again. 'And say you're sorry for sending me off that time.'

Father gave Dilly a very hard look. Dilly didn't bat an eyelid.

'Only if *you* promise to behave when you play football in future,' said Father at last. Dilly gave *him* a hard look, then nodded. 'Right, I'm *sorry*,' said Father through gritted teeth. 'Now, do you think you could you get on with it?'

'OK, Father,' Dilly replied as the striker started his run.

Then Dilly opened his mouth, and let rip with an incredibly focused, ultra-special, 150-mile-per-hour super-scream, the kind that might make a certain striker boot the ball high over the bar. And that's just what he did!

There was a HUGE roar from the crowd, and in all the excitement, nobody seemed to connect Dilly's scream with what had happened.

But we know the truth, don't we?

The referee blew his whistle for the end of the game, and the Dino-Town United supporters went wild with joy. There are no prizes for guessing which particular supporter went the wildest.

Father was so happy, he kept hugging Dilly and giving Mother big, slobbery kisses. He hugged me too, and promised to raise *my* pocket money and buy *me* a Dino-Town United outfit. It really was quite a day.

'And, er . . . thanks, Dilly,' said Father as we were leaving the stadium.

'Whatever for, Father?' said Dilly, an innocent look on his face.

'Oh, I don't know,' said Father, grinning. 'Just for being you, I suppose.'

Then we all went home to celebrate!

4 Dilly and the sleepover party

You know how it is sometimes when everything seems to be going wrong? Well, that's definitely what life was like for us a while ago. I couldn't believe it! Hardly a moment went by without another disaster.

As you can probably imagine, we weren't a happy family. In fact, there was one Monday evening when Mother, Father and I were particularly fed up.

'Oof!' said Mother, collapsing wearily into the nearest armchair. She had just come in, and hadn't even taken off her coat. *'Please* don't ask me what kind of day I've had.

Honestly, you don't want to know.'

'If it was anything like mine, you'll be needing this,' said Father, giving her a steaming-hot cup of fern-leaf tea. He flopped into the armchair next to her. 'I think Dorla's had a bad day too, haven't you, love?'

'I don't want to talk about it,' I muttered gloomily.

'Never mind, Dorla,' said Mother, and sipped her tea. 'We should get some peace and quiet at the weekend, anyway. I certainly intend to forget my troubles and relax. There's nothing special happening, is there?'

'I hope you haven't forgotten my sleep-over party, Mother,' said Dilly, suddenly appearing at the door. He had a rather fierce look on his face.

A horrified silence descended on the rest of us.

'Ah . . . no, I haven't, Dilly,' Mother managed to say eventually. 'But are you positive it's *this* weekend? I thought it wasn't for ages yet.'

'It *is* this weekend, Mother,' said Dilly sternly. 'And I can prove it.'

Dilly pointed at Saturday's date on the calendar, and there it was, in Mother's neat writing: *Dilly's sleepover party*. Father went pale green and sank deeper into his armchair. Mother let slip a little groan. I just felt sick.

I know what sleepover parties are like. I've been to plenty. They can be wild even when they involve sensible young dinosaurs of my age. So there was no telling *what* Dilly and his excitable friends might get up to.

It was a nightmare too awful to contemplate.

'He's right, you know,' Father whispered

to Mother.

'Of course I'm right,' Dilly snapped. 'You *promised*.'

'Maybe we did, Dilly,' Mother said softly in that I'm-being-gentle-because-you'll-hate-what-you're-going-to-hear tone of voice. 'But your Father and are I very tired, so can we postpone it for the time being?'

Dilly didn't say anything. He just scowled at Mother, then opened his mouth like he does when he's about to fire off a an ultra-special, 150-mile-per-hour super-scream.

Mother and Father sat up instantly.

'OK, Dilly,' said Father quickly. 'We'll take that as a no.'

'So am I having my sleepover party or not?' Dilly asked.

'Yes, Dilly, you are,' sighed Mother. 'Although we must be crazy.'

I couldn't have agreed more.

Not that anybody was interested in my opinion, least of all my little brother. Dilly had already run off. He headed straight for the dino-phone to call Denzil, Delbert, Dudley and Darryl, the friends he wanted to invite.

Dilly's been playing with the four of them a lot recently, and when the entire gang is together, Father calls them the Fearsome Five. That ought to give you some idea of what was in store for us.

Dilly didn't waste any time in his preparations. He came to breakfast the very next morning with a long list. It covered all the things he wanted Mother and Father to buy, or get hold of, for his sleepover party.

'I'm sorry, Dilly,' said Father, 'but I'm afraid I won't be able to rent any of these videos for you and your friends. I don't think *I'm* old enough myself to watch movies like *Slaughter in the Swamp* and *Dinocop*.'

'But that's not fair!' said Dilly, crossly. 'Donny had them both at his birthday party, and loads of others that were much more scary.'

'Did he now?' said Mother, frowning. 'I think I'd better have a word with Donny's parents, then. And I'm not sure about some of this other stuff, either, Dilly. Dino-Pop always makes you totally hyperactive.'

'I *know*, Mother,' said Dilly as if she were stupid. '*That's* why I want it.'

'Oh, really?' said Mother, with a you'll-be-lucky look on her face. 'I think we'll discuss this at dinner, Dilly. I mustn't be late for work.'

The conversation did resume later. It continued, on and off, for the next few days. Mother and Father gave in on some things, but not on others.

Dilly seemed pretty pleased, though. He said he had the whole of his sleepover planned. Mother and Father insisted he tell them what he was going to do. But it was obvious he didn't reveal everything.

I could see that made Mother and Father rather nervous. Actually I was sure they were absolutely *dreading* what was to come. I couldn't blame them. I was probably even more worried than they were.

Saturday arrived far too soon. Dilly's friends were due at seven in the evening, and he spent the whole afternoon staring at the clock.

'They're here!' he yelled at last, and dashed to the front door.

He pulled it open, and his friends came tumbling in, one after the other. They were all carrying sleeping-bags and rucksacks, for their pyjamas and toothbrushes, I supposed. And they were all hysterically excited. They laughed and yelled and leaped around, and they THUNDERED! up the stairs to Dilly's bedroom and slammed the door with a huge SLAM! Then they came out and THUNDERED! back downstairs again.

'Well, I think you're very brave to be doing this,' Denzil's dad said to Mother and

Father as the Fearsome Five charged into the kitchen. He was trying not to laugh. 'I only hope you make it through the night alive.'

Mother and Father smiled thinly. They didn't think it was very funny, and neither did I. But a sudden CRASH! in the kitchen distracted us.

Dilly's sleepover party had begun.

Many more things went CRASH! during that evening. The Fearsome Five raced all over the house playing wild games and having food fights. Even without drinking any Dino-Pop, Dilly was totally hyperactive.

It was almost two o'clock in the morning before Mother and Father finally managed to pen the gang in Dilly's room. They leaped into their sleeping-bags and yelled at Mother, Father and me to leave.

Ah-ha, I thought. They were *definitely* up to something.

Mother and Father weren't bothered, though. They looked shattered and seemed grateful to crawl off to their bedroom. They said goodnight to the Fearsome Five, then kissed me goodnight as well.

I snuggled down in bed, and waited. I felt sure the fun for Dilly wasn't over yet. But the house was quiet, and I was tired too. Before long I was drifting into sleep, and a lovely dream about not having a little brother.

Suddenly I was woken by the ear-splitting sound of an ultra-special, 150-mile-per-hour super-scream, the kind that seems much louder because it's night time, and sends Mother, Father and me running to Dilly's room.

'What on earth is going on?' said Mother.

It was dark in the room, and at first I couldn't see anything. Then I realised Dilly and his friends had become the *Frightened* Five. They were in a corner, hugging each other tightly, sobbing and howling with terror.

It took ages to find out the truth. What Dilly hadn't told Mother and Father was that his plan for the evening included a late-night, Incredibly Creepy Story Session. And *his* story had been the scariest of the lot.

He'd come up with it by putting together all the *worst* bits of the videos he'd seen at Donny's. He won't do that again in a hurry, I thought.

'OK, what now?' said Father. 'It's too late to call their parents.'

'We'll have to calm them down somehow,' said Mother desperately.

'I know!' I said as the howling grew louder. 'If it was *scary* stories that upset them, why don't we try telling them some *happy* stories instead?'

Mother and Father looked at me as if *I* was the one who'd gone crazy. We didn't have any choice, though. We had to sit with Dilly and his friends and take turns telling stories. *Any* stories that were happy.

We soon ran out of fairy stories and book stories we remembered. We moved on to telling funny stories about our family, and they seemed to catch everybody's attention immediately – especially those involving Dilly.

So we picked the *best* bits from all the things Dilly has done. We told stories about Dilly being cheeky, Dilly playing practical jokes, Dilly causing havoc on holiday, at a pantomime, at the vet's, at the swamp.

Gradually the sobbing and howling grew quieter, and smiles began to appear on everybody's faces. The smiles turned into gales of laughter, and before long we had all started to relax. Even Mother, Father and me.

'Do you know, I haven't felt this cheerful for *months*,' I heard Mother whisper to Father. 'Perhaps we ought to take a few days off, dear.'

After that, Mother and Father couldn't *stop* telling funny family stories. If I hadn't butted in and told them Dilly and his friends had fallen fast asleep, I'm sure we'd still be there. Not that I minded much, really.

It was good to be a happy family once more.

'My sleepover party was *fantastic*, wasn't it, Mother and Father?' Dilly said in the morning when his friends had gone home.

'Well, you certainly helped us forget our troubles,' laughed Mother.

'Great!' grinned Dilly. 'Then you won't mind that I've invited everybody back to stay again next week, will you? We're going to have so much *fun*!'

Mother, Father and I looked at each other, and smiled.

As you can see, life is never, *ever* dull with Dilly!